D0160581

SIMON SPOTLIGHT

An imprint of Simon & Schuster Children's Publishing Division
1230 Avenue of the Americas, New York, New York 10020
Copyright © 2003 by Eloise Productions Inc.
Text adaptation copyright © 2003 by Simon & Schuster, Inc.

Designed by James Salerno
Special thanks to Thomas D. Adelman at Handmade Films
Manufactured in the United States of America
First Edition
2 4 6 8 10 9 7 5 3 1
ISBN 0-689-86982-7
Based on the book *Eloise at Christmastime* by Kay Thompson, drawings by Hilary Knight, published
by Simon & Schuster Books for Young Readers. Copyright © 1958 by Kay Thompson.
Copyright © renewal 1986 by Kay Thompson. Copyright © 1999 by the Estate of Kay Thompson.

ELOISE

at
Christmas

adapted by
Kate Telfeyan
based on a television screenplay by
Elizabeth Chandler

SIMON SPOTLIGHT

New York   London   Toronto   Sydney   Singapore

I am Eloise. I am six.

I live at the Plaza Hotel, which is huge and wonderful and *très élégant,* especially at Christmastime, when it's absolutely filled, filled, filled with ribbons and holly and jingle-bell cheer.

Nanny has lived with us for as long as I can remember and, next to my mother, is the person I love most in the whole world. Nanny is English and likes Christmas just as much as I do.

My Christmas list needs to be inspected at least once a day, in case I think of any additions.

I usually do.

Ooh, look—there's the Plaza Christmas tree! I love when the tree gets delivered. First I give it a thorough inspection and tell everyone what needs to be fixed. Then I re-inspect it after it's been decorated. And . . .

Ta-da! It usually needs more tinsel, but otherwise—*très magnifique!*

Everyone knows it's just not Christmas without a little caroling!

Jingle bells, jingle bells, jingle all the way.
Oh, what fun it is to ride
in a one-horse open sleigh! . . .

You know what else I love
about Christmas? SNOW!
It absolutely has to snow at
Christmastime or else
it doesn't feel right.

Shopping is another one of my favorite things about Christmas. I always pack a very large excursion bag. You never know what you might need, for Lord's sake. I love to go to Saks Fifth Avenue. They do such a beautiful job with the wrapping!

I usually buy so many presents that it takes a whole army of bellhops to carry them up to my room.

Giving out presents can take a long time, so I try to be speedy, speedy, speedy!

"Excuse me. Did you happen to see any packages arrive? Preferably *large* ones, addressed to me—*Eloise?*"

Next to opening presents, the absolutely best part of Christmas is decorating the tree with Nanny. It's not as grand as the one in the lobby, but I love it. My dog, Weenie, and I like to hang all the ornaments while Nanny dances around singing Christmas songs at the top of her lungs.

Preparing for Christmas can be exhausting. That's why Nanny and I like to relax by the fire, cozy, cozy, cozy.

When Christmas actually arrives the Plaza is absolutely filled, filled, filled with holiday cheer, and under the tree there are so many presents to open!

But do you know what the best present of all is? Spending Christmas with my mother.